For Sophie

Jan Ormerod

# Moonlight

Puffin Books

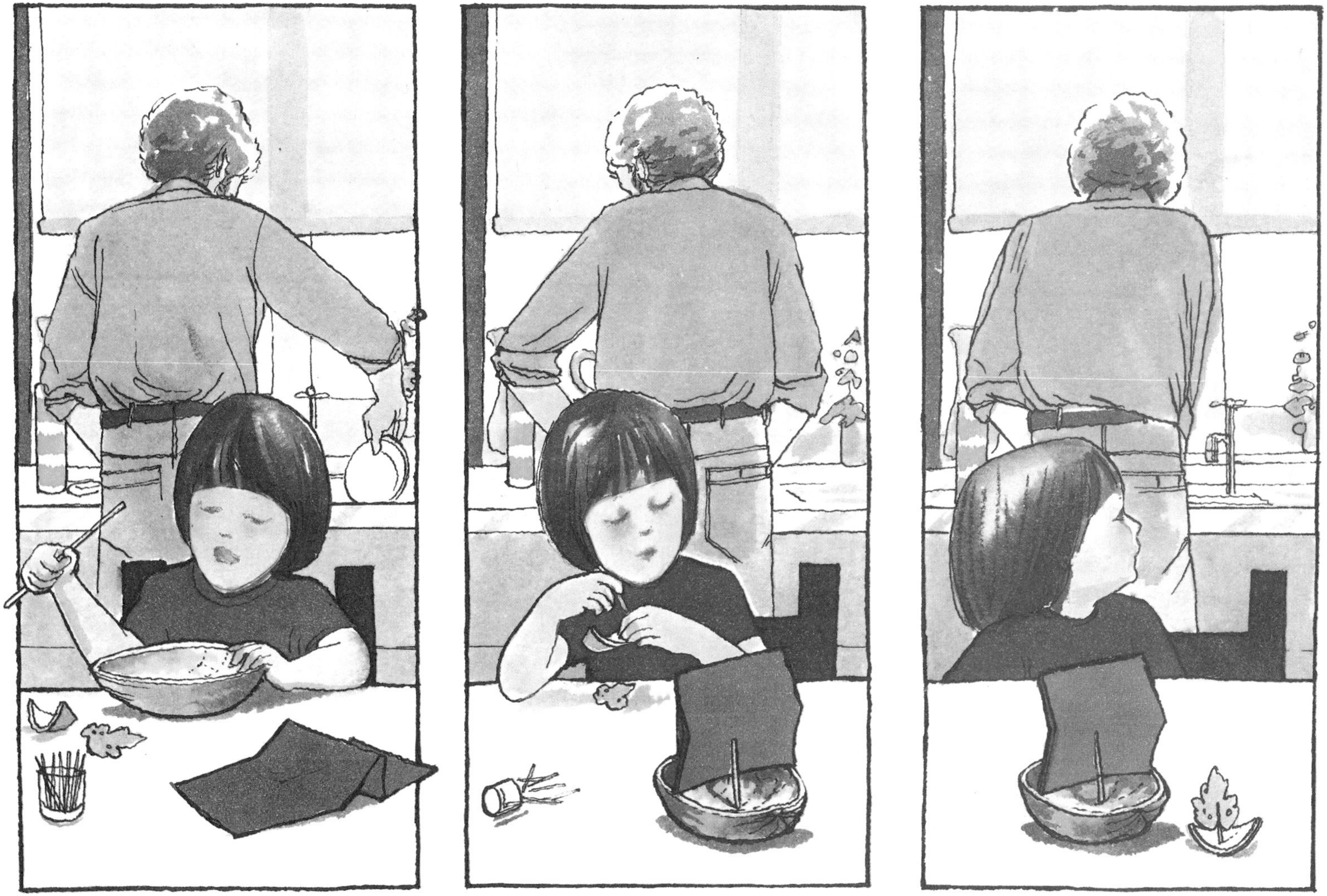

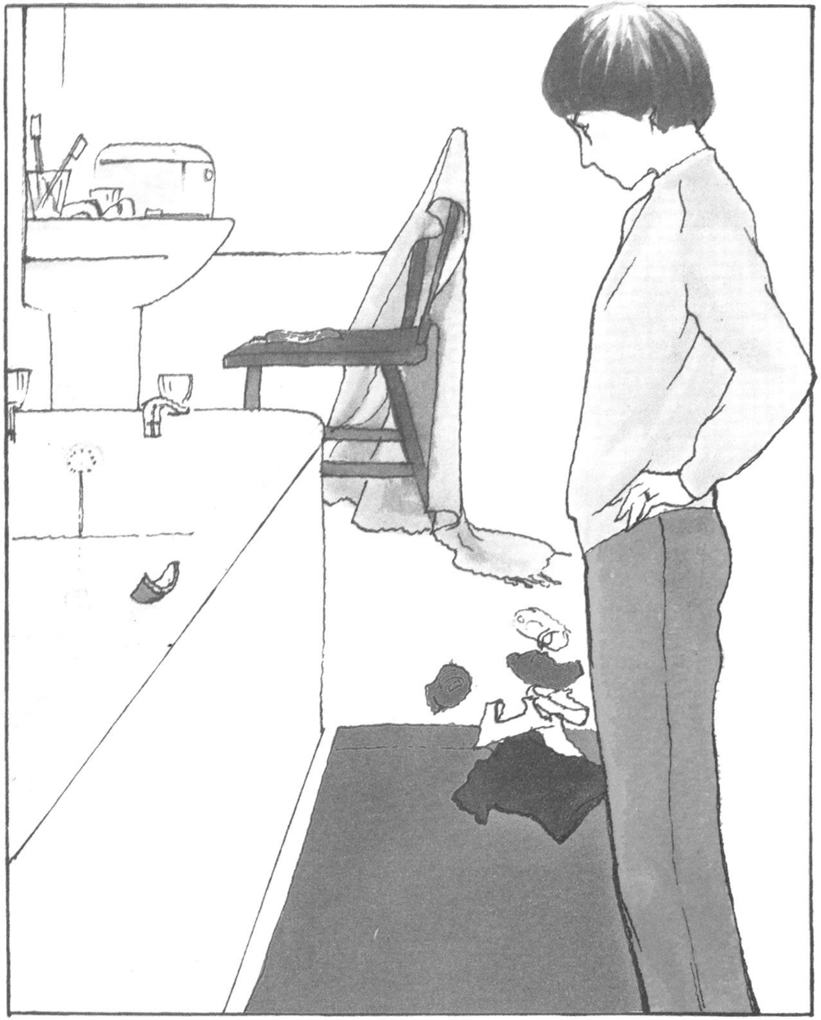

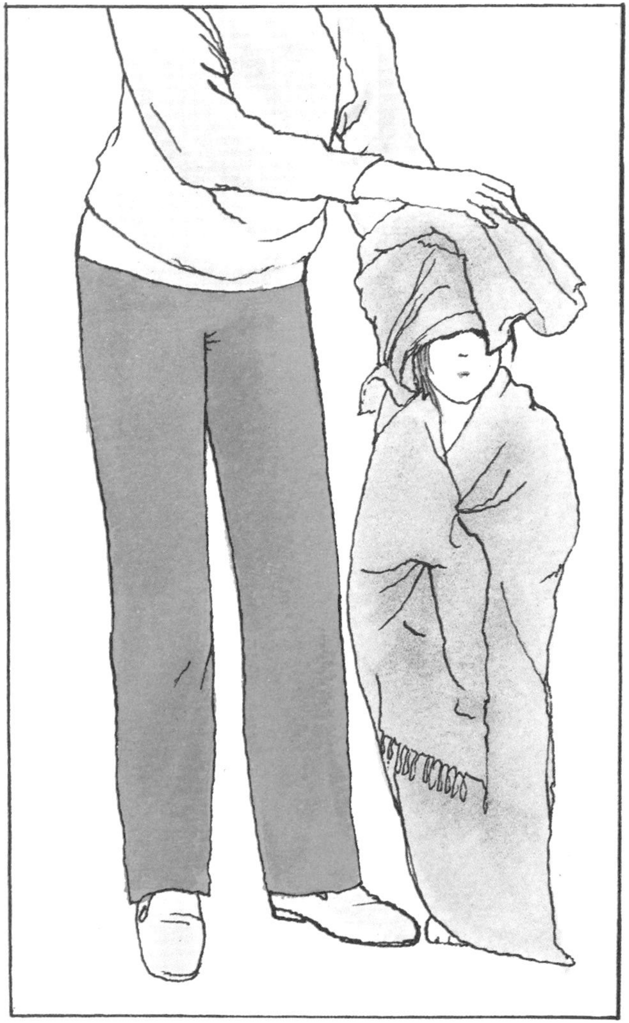

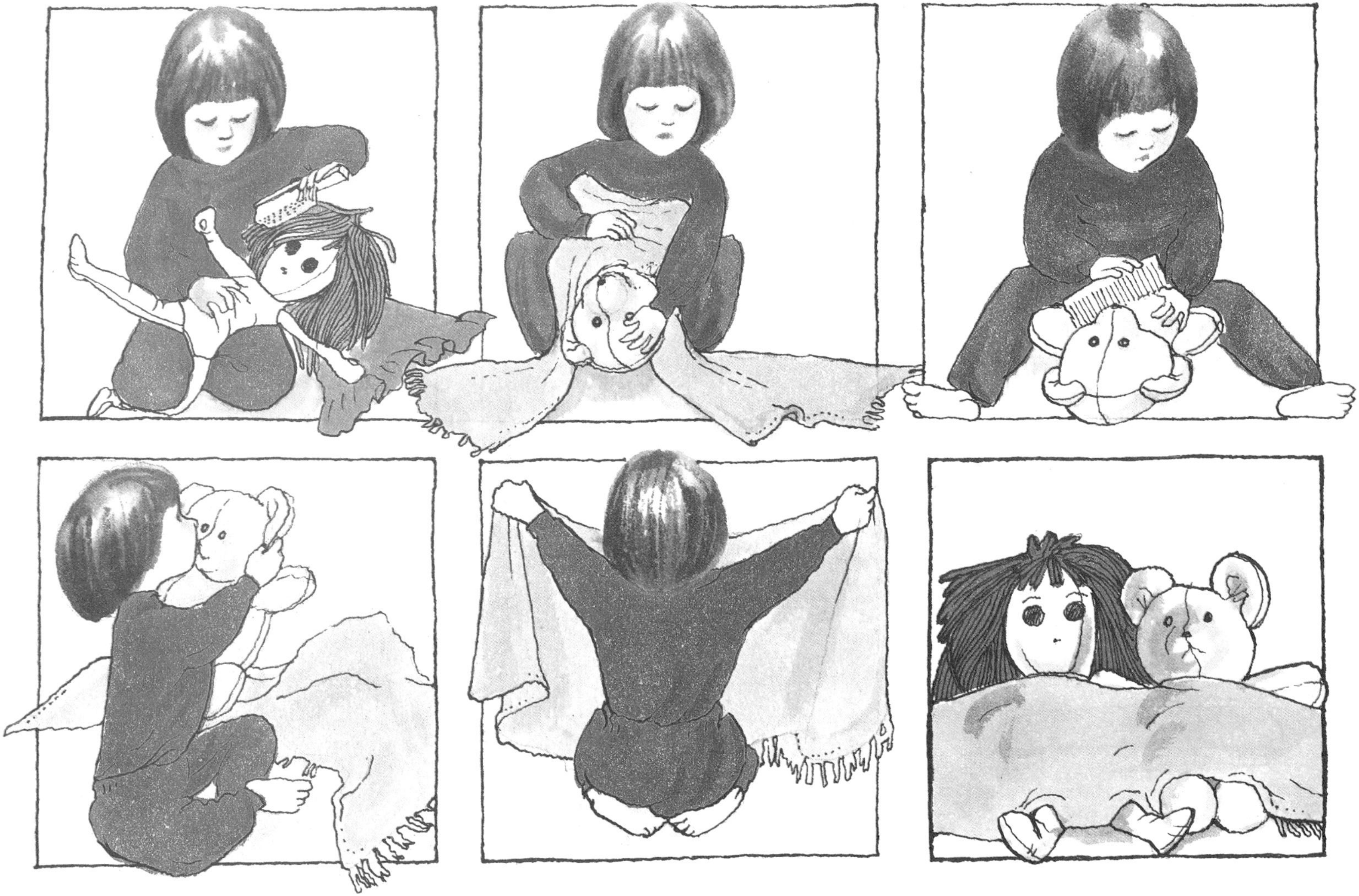

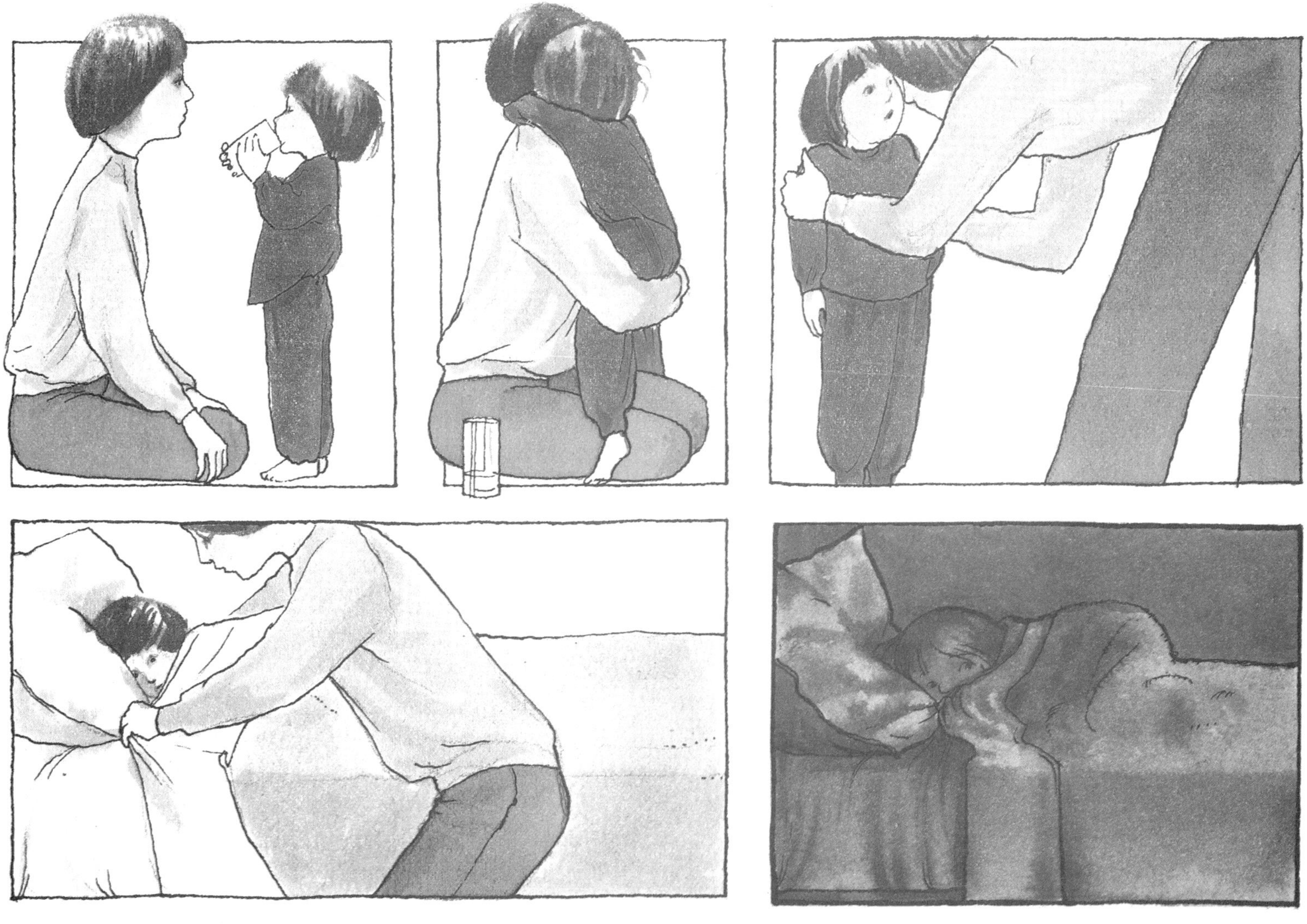

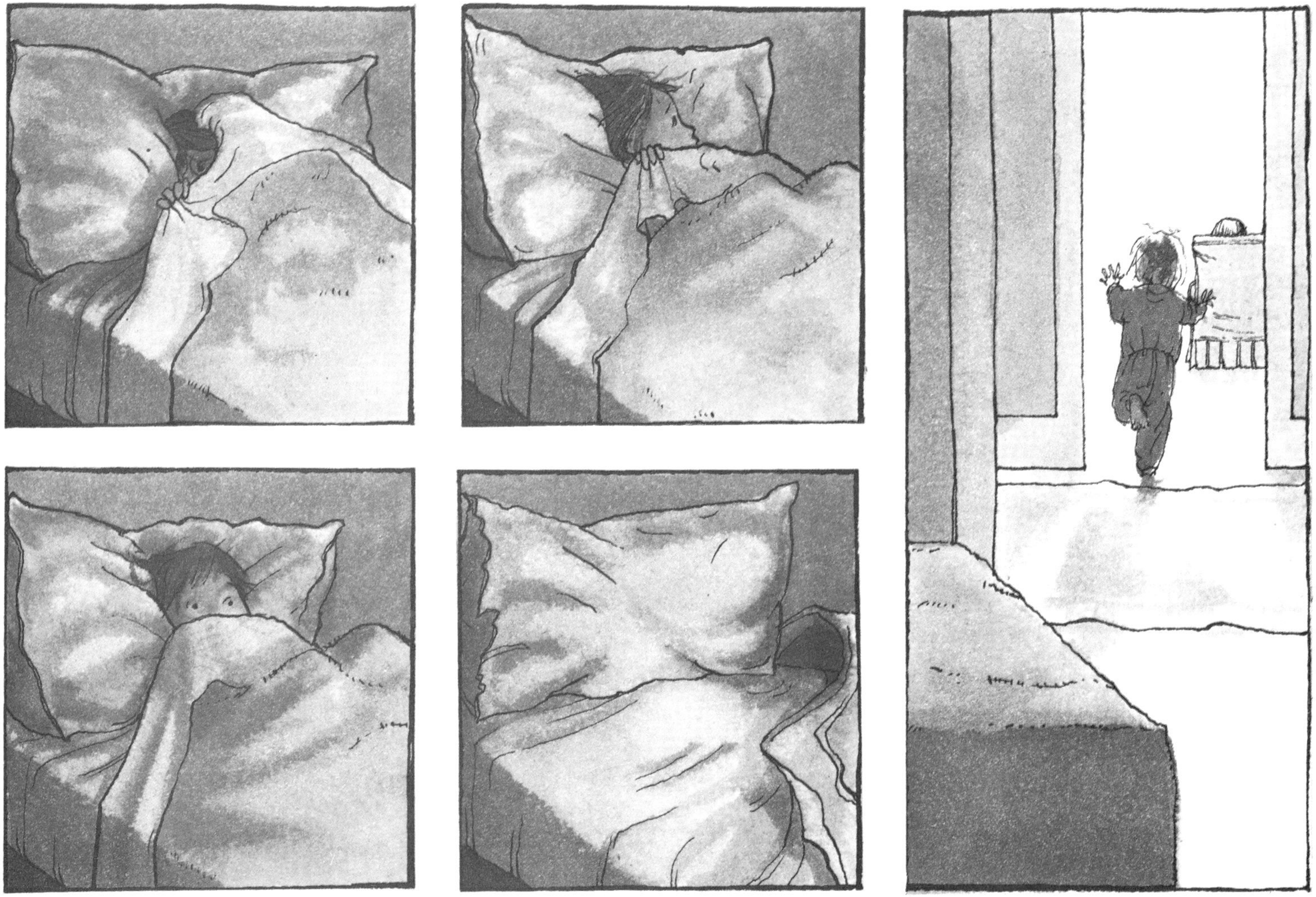

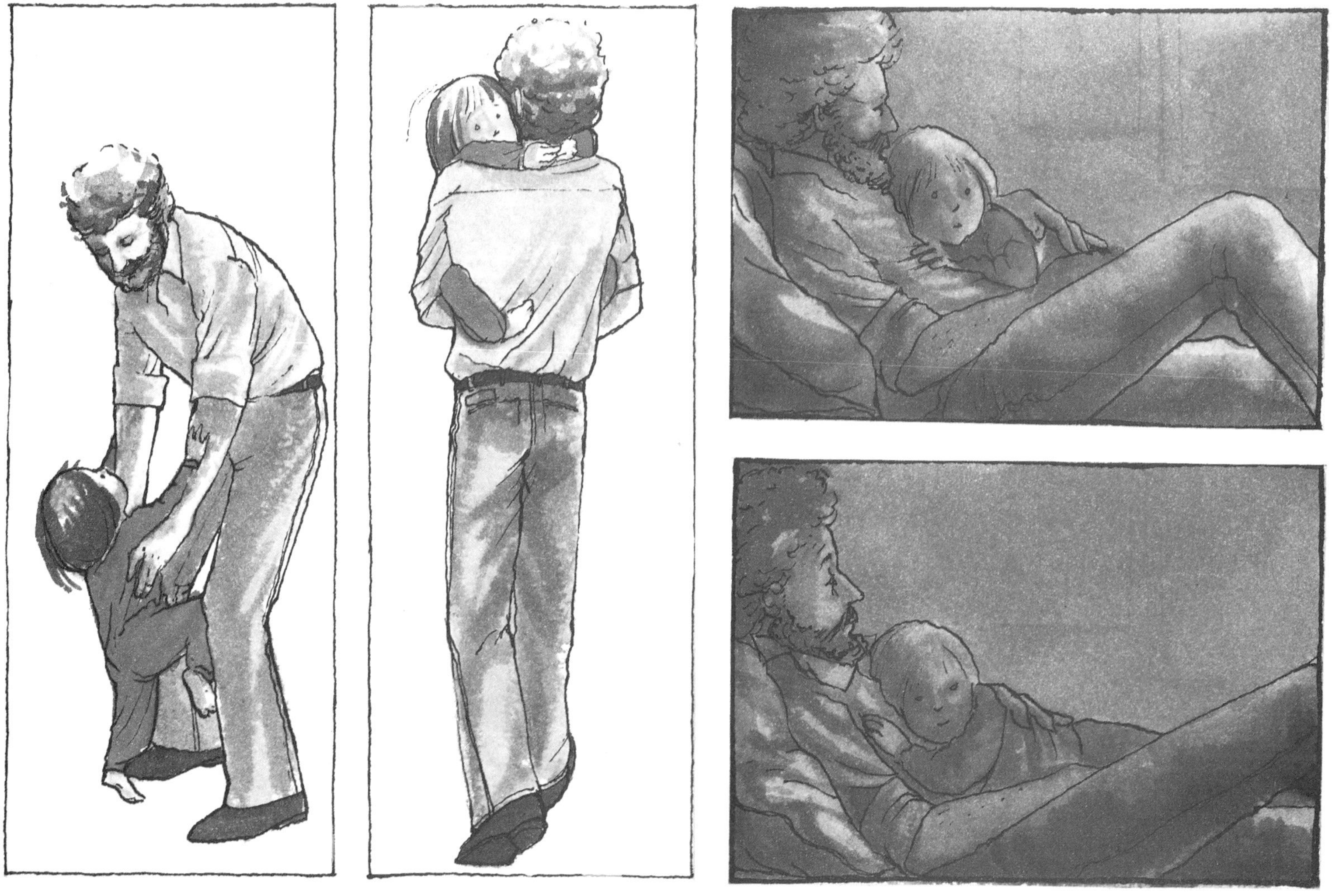

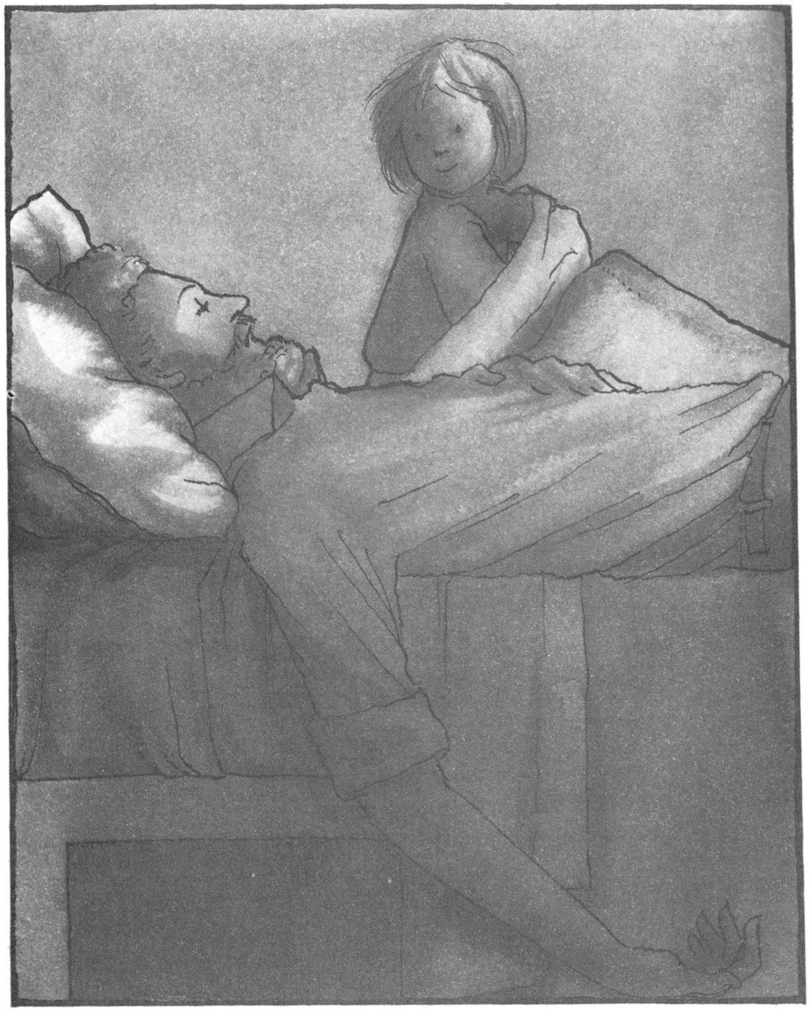

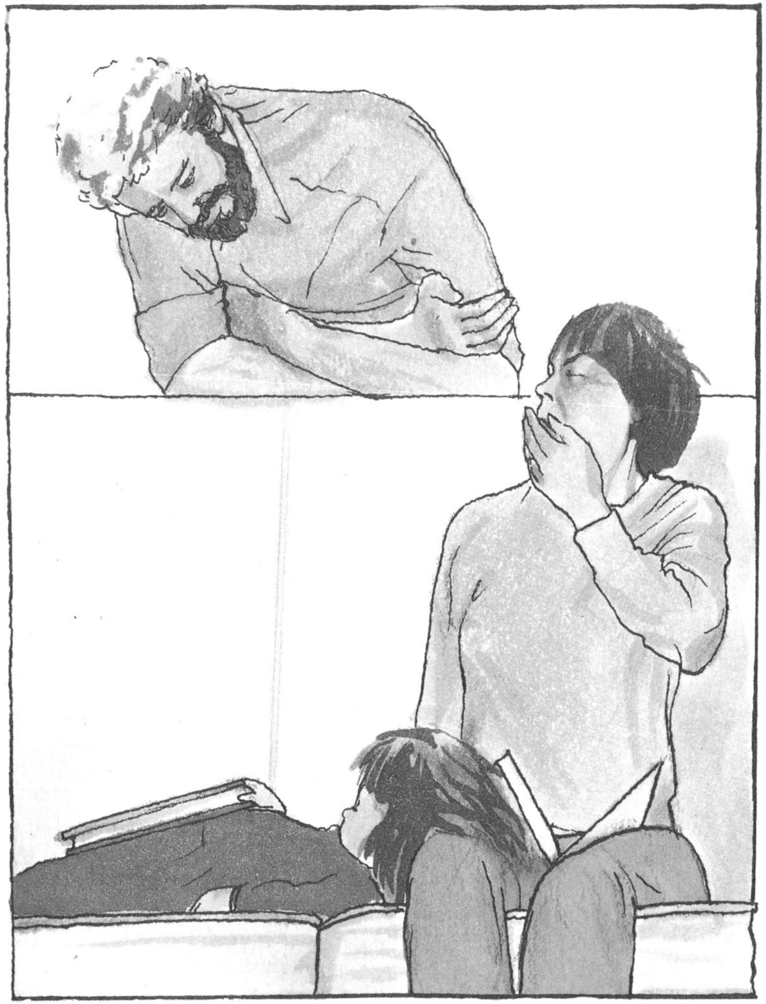

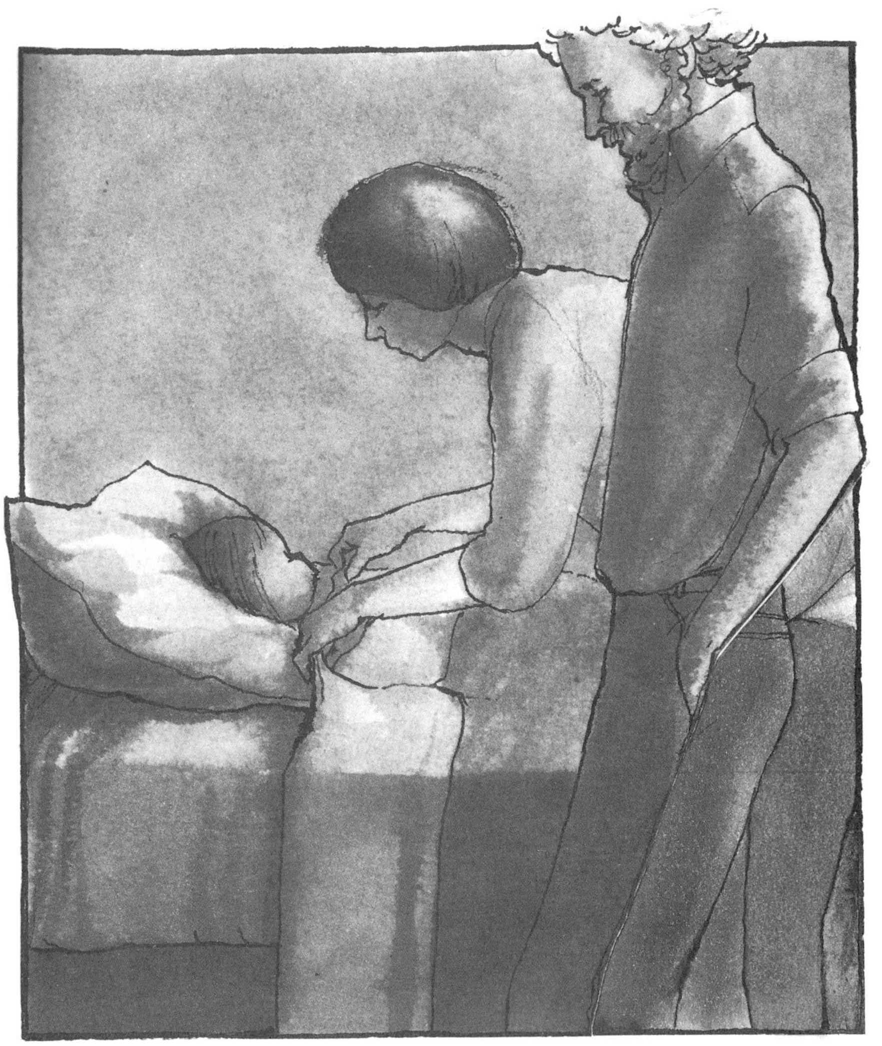

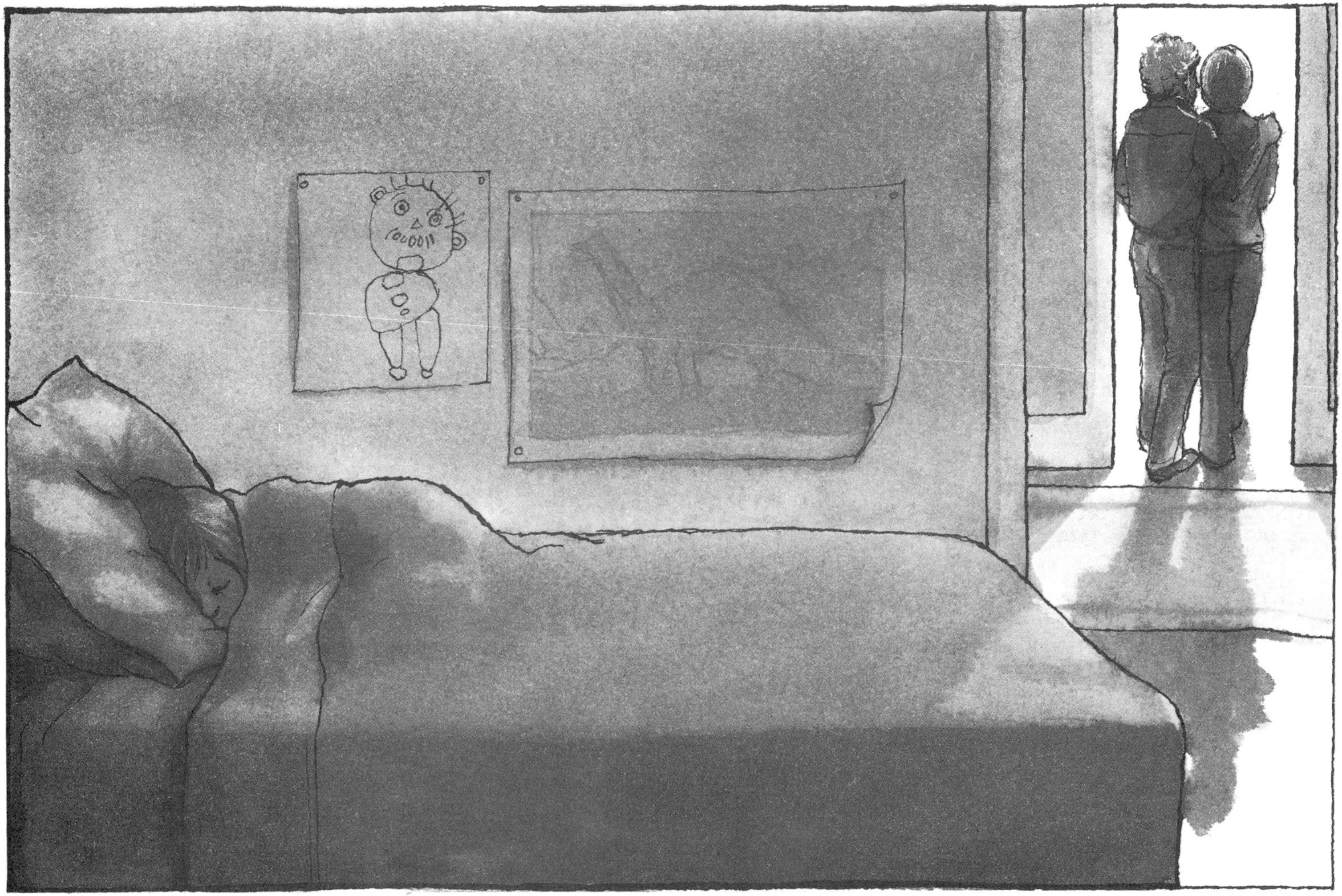